WINTER PUBLIC LIBRARY
WINTER, WI 54896

DISASTER WATCH

TSUNAMIS

Paul Mason

A+

This edition first published in 2012 in the United States of America by Smart Apple Media.
All rights reserved. No part of this book may be reproduced in any form or by any means
without written permission from the publisher.

Smart Apple Media
P.O. Box 3263
Mankato, MN, 56002

First published in 2011 by
MACMILLAN EDUCATION AUSTRALIA PTY LTD
15–19 Claremont St, South Yarra, Australia 3141

Visit our web site at www.macmillan.com.au or go directly to www.macmillanlibrary.com.au

Associated companies and representatives throughout the world.

Copyright text © Macmillan Publishers Australia 2011

Library of Congress Cataloging-in-Publication Data has been applied for.

Publisher: Carmel Heron
Commissioning Editor: Niki Horin
Managing Editor: Vanessa Lanaway
Editors: Philip Bryan and Tim Clarke
Proofreader: Kylie Cockle
Designer: Cristina Neri, Canary Graphic Design
Page layout: Cristina Neri, Canary Graphic Design
Photo researcher: Jes Senbergs (management: Debbie Gallagher)
Illustrator: Peter Bull Art Studio
Production Controller: Vanessa Johnson

Manufactured in China by Macmillan Production (Asia) Ltd.
Kwun Tong, Kowloon, Hong Kong
Supplier Code: CP January 2011

Acknowledgments
The Publisher would like to thank the Victoria State Emergency Service for their assistance in reviewing these manuscripts.

The author and publisher are grateful to the following for permission to reproduce copyright material:

Front cover photograph: Simulated tsunami on a city, courtesy of Shutterstock/Fouguin.

Photographs courtesy of: AAP Image, p. **27**, / AFP Photo/Joanne Davis, **26**; Corbis, **10**, **14**, /Franck Robichon/ epa, **23**, /Norbert Wu/Science Faction, **20** (top); Getty Images/AFP, **5**, **7**, **6**, **17**, **20** (bottom), **24**, **29**, /Shaul Schwarz/Stringer, **28**; Rob Gilley Photos, **11**; iStockPhoto/Eric Gevaert, **25**, /Daniel Stein, **22**; Photolibrary/ Mary Plage, **4**; Reuters/Stringer Indonesia, **19**, **21**, /Surkee Sukplang, **15**; Wikipedia, **12**.

While every care has been taken to trace and acknowledge copyright, the publisher tenders their apologies for any accidental infringement where copyright has proved untraceable. They would be pleased to come to a suitable arrangement with the rightful owner in each case.

The information provided in this book is general and in no way represents advice to the reader. The author and publisher take no responsibility for individual decisions made in response to information contained in this book.

Please Note
At the time of printing, the Internet addresses appearing in this book were correct. Owing to the dynamic nature of the Internet, however, we cannot guarantee that all these addresses will remain correct.

CONTENTS

Disaster Watch	4
Tsunamis	5
Where Do Tsunamis Happen?	6
What Causes Tsunamis?	8
What Is a Tsunami Like at Sea?	10
What Happens When a Tsunami Approaches Shore?	12
What Damage Do Tsunamis Cause?	14
Forecasting Tsunamis	16
Monitoring Tsunamis	18
Before a Tsunami Strikes	20
Are You at Risk?	22
Top Tips for Reducing Risk	24
What You Can Do if a Tsunami Happens	26
After a Tsunami	28
Quiz: Do You Know What to Do?	30
Disaster Watching on the Web	31
Index	32

DISASTER WORDS

When a word is printed in **bold**, look for its meaning in the "Disaster Words" box.

DISASTER WATCH

Natural disasters can destroy whole areas and kill thousands of people. The only protection from them is to go on disaster watch. This means knowing the warning signs that a disaster might be about to happen, and having a plan for what to do if one strikes.

We cannot stop natural disasters from happening, but being prepared can help reduce the harm caused by a disaster.

What Are Natural Disasters?

Natural disasters are nature's most damaging events. They include wildfires, earthquakes, extreme storms, floods, tsunamis (say *soon-ah-meez*), and volcanic eruptions.

Preparing for Natural Disasters

Preparing for natural disasters helps us to reduce their effects in three key ways, by:
- increasing our chances of survival
- making our homes as disaster-proof as possible
- reducing the long-term effects of the disaster.

TSUNAMIS

A tsunami is a giant wave. Tsunamis strike very suddenly and can cause terrible destruction in coastal regions. People who are prepared have a much better chance of surviving than people who do not know how to react.

What Is a Tsunami?

A tsunami is an ocean wave or group of waves caused by a giant movement of the seabed, usually an earthquake. The tsunami waves travel across the ocean at high speed. When the tsunami reaches land, the waves increase in size and crash ashore, causing terrible damage to low-lying coastal areas.

EYEWITNESS WORDS

Simon Clark was in Thailand and witnessed the 2004 Indian Ocean tsunami:

"Suddenly a huge wave came ... destroying everything. People who were snorkeling were dragged along the coral and washed up on the beach, and people who were sunbathing got washed into the sea."

Preparing for a Tsunami

There are three key ways to prepare for a tsunami. You must know:
- the warning signs that a tsunami is about to arrive, and what to do
- the safest places to be if a tsunami threatens
- the challenges facing those who survive a tsunami.

Vacationers and locals watched in horror as a tsunami approached the coast of Thailand in December 2004.

WHERE DO TSUNAMIS HAPPEN?

Tsunamis can affect almost any ocean coastline. They can travel a long way, and regularly affect coastlines thousands of miles from where they began. They most often damage coastal communities around the edge of the Pacific Ocean.

Where Tsunamis Begin

Tsunamis are usually created in areas where earthquakes and volcanoes are common, around the edge of the Pacific Ocean. Roughly 80 percent of tsunamis are created in the Pacific Ocean, but they are also created in the Indian and Atlantic oceans. Even smaller seas are not safe: a tsunami was recorded in the Mediterranean Sea more than 2,300 years ago.

The Seven Deadliest Tsunamis

Rank	Year	Created	Area Affected	Estimated Casualties
1	2004	Indian Ocean	Indian Ocean	230,210+**
2	1755	Atlantic Ocean	Portugal, Spain, Morocco, Ireland, UK	100,000+
3	1908	Mediterranean Sea	Messina, Italy	100,000+
4	1883	Sunda Strait	Indonesia	36,000*
5	1707	Philippine Sea	Tokaido, Japan	30,000**
6	1826	Philippine Sea	Japan	27,000
7	1868	Eastern Pacific Ocean	Africa, Chile	25,000+

*combined casualties of tsunami and volcanic eruption
**combined tsunami and earthquake   + = more than

This map shows the areas affected by the 2004 Indian Ocean tsunami, which was the world's deadliest tsunami. The waves radiated out from a powerful earthquake off the north-west coast of Indonesia.

The 2004 Indian Ocean tsunami destroyed coastal towns such as Aceh, Indonesia.

Where Tsunamis Hit

Countries around the coast of the Pacific Ocean are affected by tsunamis more often than anywhere else. Japan has been hit by almost 200 damaging tsunamis. The Pacific Ocean coastlines of North and South America are also regularly hit by tsunamis, as are the Philippines and many Pacific islands.

Where Tsunamis Cause the Most Damage

Tsunamis cause the most damage when they hit coastlines that are heavily populated. In 1964, a powerful tsunami formed off the coast of Alaska, United States. Despite being created by a more powerful earthquake than the 2004 Indian Ocean tsunami, it killed fewer than 131 people. This is because there were few people living in the area.

The Indian Ocean Tsunami

Date: December 26, 2004
Location: Indian Ocean

The 2004 Indian Ocean tsunami is the most destructive tsunami ever recorded. It began without warning early in the morning of December 26. By the end of the day, it had hit crowded beaches right across the Indian Ocean. The tsunami and its aftermath killed more than 200,000 people.

WHAT CAUSES TSUNAMIS?

The most powerful tsunamis are caused by earthquakes. These tsunamis are capable of crossing whole oceans very quickly. Undersea volcanic eruptions and landslides can also cause tsunamis, but these do not usually travel long distances.

Earthquakes

Earth's crust is covered with **tectonic plates**. During an earthquake, the tectonic plates under the sea suddenly move. This sudden move disturbs the water above the tectonic plates and causes a tsunami. The bigger the earthquake, the bigger the tsunami produced. In December 2004, the Indian Ocean tsunami was caused by one of the biggest earthquakes ever recorded. The result was a tsunami that in places was more than 98 feet (30 m) high when it reached the shore.

DISASTER WORDS

tectonic plates giant sheets of rock that make up Earth's surface

Tsunami Speed

The 2004 Indian Ocean tsunami began just before 7.00 A.M. local time, off the northwest coast of Sumatra, Indonesia. The wave sped across the ocean and:
- after 10 minutes, it hit Sumatra
- after one hour, it reached Thailand
- after two hours, it arrived in Sri Lanka
- after seven hours, it hit the coast of East Africa.

A massive earthquake caused the 2004 Indian Ocean tsunami. Each colored band represents the distance traveled by the tsunami in half an hour.

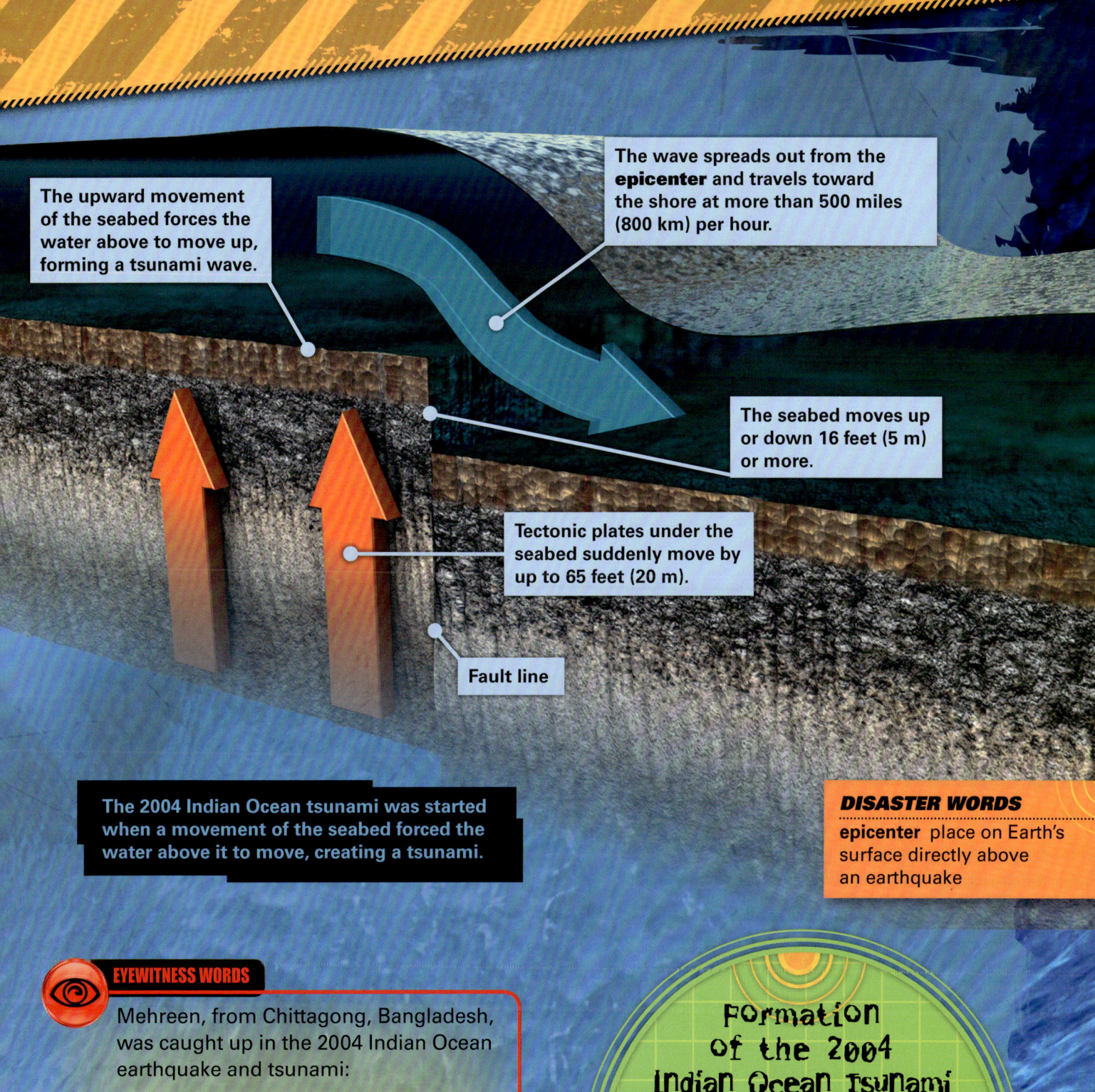

The upward movement of the seabed forces the water above to move up, forming a tsunami wave.

The wave spreads out from the **epicenter** and travels toward the shore at more than 500 miles (800 km) per hour.

The seabed moves up or down 16 feet (5 m) or more.

Tectonic plates under the seabed suddenly move by up to 65 feet (20 m).

Fault line

The 2004 Indian Ocean tsunami was started when a movement of the seabed forced the water above it to move, creating a tsunami.

DISASTER WORDS
epicenter place on Earth's surface directly above an earthquake

EYEWITNESS WORDS

Mehreen, from Chittagong, Bangladesh, was caught up in the 2004 Indian Ocean earthquake and tsunami:

"Me and my sister were near the port when we felt a sudden movement beneath our feet. We then saw people screaming and running away from the coast. There were huge waves …. It was as if the sea was swallowing the land."

Formation of the 2004 Indian Ocean Tsunami

The 2004 Indian Ocean tsunami shows how earthquakes create tsunamis. The earthquake happened under the seabed off the coast of Sumatra, Indonesia. It lasted almost 10 minutes, and was so powerful that Earth vibrated almost half an inch (up to 1 cm).

WHAT IS A TSUNAMI LIKE AT SEA?

Tsunamis look different depending on the depth of water they are traveling through. In deep water, a tsunami can be impossible to spot, but as it nears the coast the wave becomes easier to see.

DISASTER WORDS
wind-generated made by the wind

Tsunamis in Deep Water

As they travel across deep oceans, even the most powerful tsunamis might be only 3 feet (1 m) high, or even less. This is smaller than most **wind-generated** waves. This means that tsunamis are unlikely to be seen with the naked eye. Specialist equipment is needed to detect tsunamis as they move across deep oceans toward land.

Deep-water tsunamis have struck the island of Hawaii many times, causing widespread devastation. This photograph shows the wreckage after a tsunami hit the city of Hilo in 1949.

The Hilo Tsunamis

Dates: April 1, 1946 and May 23, 1960
Location: Hawaiian Islands

The Hawaiian city of Hilo has been hit by two major tsunamis. In 1946, the tsunami hit without warning and 159 people died. In 1960, warning sirens went off but some people ignored them: 61 people died.

In deep water, the wave is visible only as a raised line in the ocean's surface.

As the wave gets into less-deep water, it slows down and grows bigger.

When the wave reaches shallow water, its top begins to foam and the wave may break.

As they reach shallow water, these waves behave in a similar way to a tsunami, but much less extreme.

Tsunamis in Shallow Water

As tsunamis get close to shore, their size and speed change.

Change in Size

As it reaches shallower water, a tsunami wave gets bigger. If the sea is shallow a long way from shore, the tsunami will be visible as a line of water coming toward land. It rushes forward like a huge **high tide**.

Change in Speed

Shallow water makes tsunamis slow down. A tsunami's speed can drop to ten percent of its maximum speed, from more than 500 miles (800 km) per hour to 50 miles (80 km) per hour, or less.

DISASTER WORDS
high tide greatest height the sea normally reaches

11

WHAT HAPPENS WHEN A TSUNAMI APPROACHES SHORE?

As a tsunami approaches shore, it grows in size and changes shape. Exactly how the tsunami behaves as it reaches land depends on the type and size of the tsunami, and on the shape of the coastline.

Types of Tsunami

When two **tectonic plates** meet, they form a line called a **fault line**. An earthquake under the seabed lifts the plates along that fault line and creates a tsunami on each side: one tsunami with a hollow or **trough** of water in front of it, and another without.

Tsunamis with a Trough

When a tectonic plate drops down during an earthquake, the sea surface above it also drops, creating a tsunami with a **trough**. As the wave moves away, the trough moves in front of it, reaching the shore ahead of the wave. The first tsunami warning many people get is when they see the sea level drop unusually low.

DISASTER WORDS

tectonic plates giant sheets of rock that make up Earth's surface
fault line place where two tectonic plates meet
trough dip or lower area

EYEWITNESS WORDS

Bernadette Malinson described a series of tsunami waves that hit New Zealand after the 2010 Chilean earthquake:

"The bay empties right out. It takes about a minute and a half and then it surges back in …. The surges have been getting bigger – at least 6 feet (2 m) at present."

Seconds before a tsunami hits, the ocean that covered the beach draws back to expose the sand.

Tsunamis without a Trough

A tsunami without a trough hits the shore without any visible warnings. In the 2004 Indian Ocean tsunami, there was no trough of water on the wave that traveled toward the coast of Africa, so it took people completely by surprise.

A tsunami forms on both sides of a plate movement, but only one side has a trough.

The Shape of the Coastline

Tsunamis are affected by the shape of the coastline. Where the coastline narrows, tsunamis heading straight ashore will grow larger. Steep-sided bays, river mouths, or harbors can push the water inward and increase their size even farther. For example, the tsunami waves that hit Hilo Bay in Hawaii in 1960 reached more than 32 feet (10 m), which was double the height they reached anywhere else.

Breaking Waves

Only the largest tsunami waves actually break. Most simply come ashore as a fast-moving, ever-rising wall of water, which peaks at a **run-up**.

DISASTER WORDS
run-up highest point reached by a wave

WHAT DAMAGE DO TSUNAMIS CAUSE?

Imagine the force of being hit in the face by a bucket of water. Now think how powerful a tsunami must be, as millions of tons of water come rushing ashore. It is no wonder that tsunamis can cause terrible damage to humans and the environment.

Human Impact

Tsunamis affect people in two key ways: by injuring and killing them, and by damaging property.

Injuring People

When a tsunami strikes, people may be killed or injured from the immediate effects of the wave. Then, after the tsunami has gone, dirty drinking water, sickness, and lack of food may cause further deaths.

Damaging Property

Tsunamis destroy homes and other buildings, leaving many people **displaced**, with nowhere to live. In 2004, for example, roughly 1.69 million people were displaced by the Indian Ocean tsunami.

DISASTER WORDS
displaced forced to move from their homes to a new area

EYEWITNESS WORDS

One eyewitness described the aftermath of the 2004 Indian Ocean tsunami in Penang, Malaysia:

"Many people have been badly injured … as a result of being tossed from vehicles, especially motorcycles, and smashed into the buildings."

In 1960, a tsunami destroyed the waterfront areas of Hilo, Hawaii, for the second time. Hilo had been rebuilt after being hit by a tsunami in 1946.

Tsunamis can wash sea turtles ashore and destroy the eggs that they lay on beaches.

Environmental Impact

Tsunamis affect the natural environment, and the people and animals that depend on it.

Damage to the Environment

The flood of water from a tsunami causes terrible damage to the natural environment. Poisonous chemicals, waste water from people's homes, and **sewage** may be washed inland. Seawater makes the freshwater supply salty, so the water can no longer be drunk. The salt kills plants that people and animals rely on.

Animals and Tsunamis

Animals near the coast may be drowned or crushed, or be unable to find food in the tsunami's aftermath. Fish and other sea creatures are washed ashore and die.

DISASTER WORDS
sewage toilet waste from people's homes

Making Tsunamis Worse

It is possible that changes to the environment made the 2004 Indian Ocean tsunami more destructive. These changes include clearing mangrove forests from coastlines and removing offshore reefs. The reefs and mangroves could have absorbed some of the force of the tsunami.

FORECASTING TSUNAMIS

We cannot predict when the earthquakes that cause tsunamis will happen, so it is not possible to predict tsunamis. However, historical information and modern scientific instruments give some idea of when a tsunami might be about to happen.

DISASTER WORDS
magnitude power or violence

Historical Information

An area's history can be used to work out when a tsunami might be due. For example, many tsunamis have hit the Japanese island Hokkaido. These include some more than 32 feet (10 m) high, which strike about every 500 years. It has been more than 500 years since such a huge tsunami hit Hokkaido – so, in theory, one is overdue.

Problems with Historical Information

Unfortunately, historical information cannot reliably predict tsunamis. The size or **magnitude** of an earthquake is measured on a scale called a Richter scale, which ranges from 1 to 8. Earthquakes with a magnitude greater than 8 rarely happen more than once a year. Three days before the 2004 Indian Ocean tsunami, there was an undersea earthquake north of Macquarie Island, Australia, which measured 8.1. So, historical predictions suggested the Indian Ocean earthquake was unlikely for at least a year.

By studying an area's history, it is possible to forecast when a tsunami may strike. In 1960, an earthquake destroyed houses in Chile (pictured) and created a tsunami that later hit Japan on the other side of the Pacific Ocean.

Seismology

Seismologists use **seismological** monitoring to work out if an undersea earthquake or volcanic eruption is on its way. If their instruments detect increased movements deep below Earth's surface, an undersea earthquake or volcanic event that could cause a tsunami might be about to happen.

Problems with Seismological Predictions

Seismological predictions are not completely reliable. Sometimes activity builds up then stops again, without an earthquake happening. At other times, undersea earthquakes happen without warning. For example, seismologists thought that the **fault line** that caused the 2004 Indian Ocean tsunami was **dormant**, but it had been building up pressure ahead of a gigantic plate movement.

The Hokkaido-Nansei Tsunami
Dates: July 12, 1993
Location: Hokkaido, Japan
The Hokkaido-Nansei tsunami was one of the biggest tsunamis to ever hit Japan. The tsunami warnings on TV and radio did not reach people in time for them to act. The wave **run-up** was 98 feet (30 m) above the sea's usual height and more than 200 people died.

Seismologists recorded an earthquake off the coast of Japan two minutes before a tsunami hit the Japanese island of Hokkaido in 1993.

DISASTER WORDS
seismologists scientists who study earthquakes
seismological earthquake-related
fault line place where two tectonic plates meet
dormant sleeping; inactive
run-up highest point reached by a wave

MONITORING TSUNAMIS

Once an undersea earthquake has happened, there are systems in place to determine whether it has caused a tsunami, and how powerful the waves might be.

DISASTER WORDS
water pressure weight of water pressing down from above

Tsunami Detection

The most advanced tsunami detection systems use buoys that measure changes in the **water pressure** on the sea floor. Ordinary waves do not affect this pressure, but tsunamis do. Once a buoy is triggered, it sends a message to a tsunami warning center telling them that a tsunami is coming.

4 Message sent to tsunami warning center

3 Message sent to satellite

A tsunami sensor is used to send messages from the seabed to the tsunami warning center.

2 Surface buoy

1 Tsunami sensor on seabed sends message to surface buoy

The 1964 Alaskan Tsunami

Date: March 29, 1964
Location: Prince William Sound, Alaska, United States

This 21-foot (6.5-m) high tsunami raced down the west coast of North America without warning, causing widespread damage. It also hit islands in the Pacific Ocean, although by the time it reached Japan, it was just 8 inches (20 cm) high.

Areas Covered by Tsunami Detection

Most tsunami-detection buoys are in the Pacific Ocean. After the 2004 Indian Ocean tsunami, plans were developed to install more buoys in the Pacific, Atlantic, and Indian oceans, and in the Caribbean Sea.

By using computers to monitor tsunamis, it is possible to predict the path that they will follow.

Monitoring Tsunami Behavior

Once a tsunami has been detected and is being monitored, computers can accurately predict when it will reach shore and how big it will be. Warnings can then be sent out, telling people to prepare for a tsunami.

Predicting Arrival Times

As tsunami waves pass by, warning buoys send signals by satellite to a central computer. The computer also knows when the earthquake that caused the tsunami began, and when it passed other buoys. It works out how fast the tsunami is traveling and when it will reach land.

Predicting Tsunami Size

The size of a tsunami is worked out from the change in water pressure as it passes a warning buoy. Computers combine this information with what they know of the shape of the ocean floor and coastline. They predict how big the tsunami will be when it reaches particular locations, and how far inland the waters will reach.

Chile Earthquake

On February 27, 2010, an earthquake near Chile sent tsunami waves across the Pacific Ocean. Tsunami-warning buoys helped provide information about the progress of the waves.

Progress of the 2010 Chile Tsunami

Location	Time Elapsed	Size of Tsunami
Talcahuano, Chile	23 minutes	9.5 ft (2.9 m)
Easter Island	5 hr 31 mins	14 in (0.35 m)
Rarotonga, Cook Islands	13 hr 16 mins	6 in (0.15 m)
San Diego, United States	13 hr 58 mins	5 in (0.13 m)
Gold Coast, Australia	19 hr 26 mins	8 in (0.2 m)

BEFORE A TSUNAMI STRIKES

When a tsunami strikes, governments and emergency services warn people to get to safe places. Next, they begin to help people, by preparing a **relief effort**.

DISASTER WORDS
relief effort help for people in difficulty

Tsunami Warnings

How much warning people get that a tsunami is coming depends on whether they are in a wealthy country or a poorer country. In wealthy countries, the warnings are usually better. This is because many of the warning systems are expensive and rely on technology that is not widely available.

Warnings in Wealthy Countries

In areas where tsunamis have struck in the past, coastal areas often have warning sirens. There are also signs warning which areas might be affected by tsunamis. It is important that these sirens and signs are heeded. In Hilo, Hawaii, in 1960, many people died because they did not take notice of the warning sirens.

Students who live in tsunami hazard areas can practice what they would do in the event of a tsunami by taking part in a tsunami warning drill.

Relief workers help victims of the 2004 Indian Ocean tsunami.

Warnings in Poorer Countries

Poorer countries may not have good enough communications to be able to warn people that a tsunami is coming. If the wave has a **trough** in front of it, the first warning is often the **drawback**. During the 2004 Indian Ocean tsunami, some local people were saved because they had heard traditional stories that a drawback was a warning that a tsunami was on its way.

DISASTER WORDS
trough dip or lower area
drawback drop in sea level before a tsunami arrives
evacuation emergency departure from a dangerous area

EYEWITNESS WORDS

Carol Noel of Hilo, Hawaii, heard the tsunami warnings on February 27, 2010:

*"The tsunami warnings went off about an hour ago to alert folks and there is **evacuation** going on in low-lying areas. Hilo expects to be hit about 11.21 this morning."*

The Indonesia Tsunami
Date: June 3, 1994
Location: Java, Indonesia

The 1994 Indonesian tsunami affected coastlines from Java to the west coast of Australia. In Java, the enormous waves hit without warning and at least 121 people died. In the Onslow-Exmouth region of Australia, the waves were smaller and warnings were issued; no one died.

Preparing for the Aftermath

As the warnings go out, the government is also preparing to deal with the aftermath of the tsunami. Hospitals, emergency services, and defense forces are told to be ready to help victims. Survivors may need medical aid, food, freshwater, and temporary shelter, so these must also be made ready.

ARE YOU AT RISK?

Are you and your family at risk from a tsunami? Your local library and council offices, and the Internet, are good places to start to investigate the area where you are living or staying.

Key Questions

Measure the risk from a tsunami by asking key questions about an area's tsunami history, and whether there are preparations in place in case a tsunami strikes. Ask the following questions about where you live, or where you are vacationing.

Are You near the Coast?

If yes, carry on your investigations. If no, a tsunami is not likely to affect you.

Has the Area Been Hit by a Tsunami before?

If a tsunami has struck before, there is a good chance that one could hit again at some time. Even if not, or if the tsunami was a very long time ago, it does not necessarily mean you are safe. Check whether there has been an earthquake or any volcanic activity in the region, as either of these could trigger a tsunami.

After Hilo in Hawaii was destroyed by tsunamis, the city was rebuilt away from the ocean, with parkland between the city and the water.

How Far above Sea Level are You?

A strong building 164 feet (50 meters) above sea level is unlikely to be damaged by a tsunami, even if it is close to the sea. However, a home 546 yards (500 m) from the ocean but only several feet above sea level could be in real danger.

Are There Any Tsunami Defenses in Place?

If the worst happens and a tsunami strikes, are there any defenses in place? For example, after Hilo, Hawaii, had been twice destroyed by tsunamis (in 1946 and 1960), the city decided that there should be no building close to the sea, and created parkland there instead. Many Japanese towns have sea walls to keep out big waves caused by extreme storms and tsunamis.

EYEWITNESS WORDS

In February, 2010, Japanese Prime Minister Yukio Hatoyama warned people to be on alert, as a tsunami that began in Chile spread across the Pacific Ocean:

"Carelessness is the biggest enemy. In the past, even if the waves were not so big, there has been great damage from 6-feet (2-m) high tsunamis."

If a coastline has a history of being hit by tsunamis, it may be necessary to build defenses. These sea defenses are on the coast at Namazu, Japan.

TOP TIPS FOR REDUCING RISK

The best way to survive a tsunami is to arm yourself with accurate information about tsunamis, and to be ready long before one arrives. Do not wait for government warnings, or for help that may not come in time. If you are living or staying where a tsunami could strike, prepare an emergency plan.

DISASTER WORDS

evacuation emergency departure from a dangerous area

Preparing an Emergency Plan

An emergency plan is a plan detailing what everyone will do if a tsunami happens. Start by discussing the plan with your family. You should aim to:
- make sure that everyone knows what the warning signals sound or look like, what they mean, and if there are different levels of warning
- identify safe places to head for when the tsunami warning goes off
- include more than one way out, or **evacuation** route, in case roads are destroyed
- practice the plan, making sure everyone knows where to meet and what to do.

The local council may be able to help. For example, the council may have already identified safe areas and evacuation routes.

Indonesian school students practice their tsunami drill to reduce the risk of anyone getting hurt should a tsunami strike.

Tsunami Myths

Believing some of these myths about tsunamis could cost you your life.

1 *A tsunami is a single wave.*

False! Almost all tsunamis arrive as a group of waves, sometimes with quite large gaps between them. Always assume another wave is coming, and that it is unsafe to be near the shore.

2 *Hanging on to a solid object will help you survive a tsunami.*

False! You are unlikely to be able to hang on against the flow of water from a tsunami.

3 *Boats can shelter from a tsunami in harbor.*

False! The safest place for boats is far out to sea, where the wave will be very small. If someone suggests heading into shore because a tsunami is coming, tell them to head to deep water instead.

Water will flow in (and out) here

Likely to be safe

May be damaged or destroyed

Poor evacuation route

Relatively safe route

Working out where a tsunami's effects are likely to be worst will help to prepare an emergency plan.

WHAT YOU CAN DO IF A TSUNAMI HAPPENS

If a tsunami strikes and you are in an area that could be affected, grab your emergency pack and head for safety immediately! Abandon your belongings, as the time spent gathering them up could cost you your life.

DISASTER WORDS

evacuate leave a dangerous place to go somewhere safer

drawback drop in sea level before a tsunami arrives

After the Warnings

What you can do to stay safe from a tsunami will depend on how much warning you have been given.

With Hours of Warning

Sometimes people have hours of warning that a tsunami is coming, and even know what time it is due. There is time to **evacuate**.

With a Few Minutes' Warning

With a few minutes' warning, you may be able to get to higher ground. If you have seen a **drawback** on the beach, run for the highest ground you can reach in one or two minutes: you will not have much longer than that.

With a few minutes' warning, the people dining at this restaurant in Phuket, Thailand, were able to escape before the 2004 Indian Ocean tsunami swept in.

With no Warning

Climb as far as possible up the sturdiest, tallest building you can find. Ideally, choose a building with something solid between it and the sea.

As a Last Resort

Climb the biggest, most solid-looking tree available. This is far from safe, as trees are often uprooted by tsunamis, but it is safer than staying on the ground.

If you find yourself caught in the water, try to grab hold of something that floats. This will keep you afloat if you are pulled out to sea as the water level drops.

EYEWITNESS WORDS

Japanese government official Yasuo Sekita warned people in February, 2010, that:

"The waves can climb up the land, so for real safety you should evacuate to a place several times higher than the predicted height of the waves."

Tsunami Emergency Kit

Keep a tsunami emergency kit somewhere obvious, where everyone knows its location and it is easy to grab quickly. It should contain food and water for at least a week, plus a first-aid kit. (Make sure you select food that will not spoil.) You could also add:
• dry, warm clothing and a waterproof cover or coat
• torch and batteries
• battery or wind-up radio
• can-opener
• enough cash for traveling and buying food for several weeks
• cell phone, ideally with a charged spare battery.

After the 2004 Indian Ocean tsunami hit Madras, India, coastguards helped to rescue people from the water by helicopter.

AFTER A TSUNAMI

The danger from a tsunami does not end when the waters recede. There may be more waves coming, perhaps bigger ones. Even when the waves have stopped, the aftermath will present other challenges to deal with.

Multiple Waves

If there are several tsunamis, it will only be clear afterward which one of them was biggest. If you can do it quickly, it is a good idea to get to a safer position after the first wave has struck, in case a bigger wave arrives. Once you have reached safer ground, stay away from the danger area for at least half a day – and longer, if possible. That way you are unlikely to be caught by any waves that arrive late.

DISASTER WORDS
recede move back

EYEWITNESS WORDS

Jayarine Saldin-lyne, from Colombo, Sri Lanka, saw the tragic results of there being more than one wave in the 2004 Indian Ocean tsunami:

"My brother-in-law and his parents had got engulfed by the 'killer' wave – the second one."

After the 2004 Indian Ocean tsunami, people searched the wreckage for anything that they could use to rebuild, such as old bricks.

After a tsunami struck Indonesia in 2005, US soldiers were sent to the affected area to provide relief to the residents.

Help after the Disaster

Once the tsunami has finally ended, help will come from two sources. The emergency services will eventually arrive with food, medical supplies, and other necessities. However, first, the survivors have to work together to help each other. Among the key things they will need are:

- food and clean drinking water. Food and clean water could be scarce, so people will need to share what they have, as drinking polluted water causes sickness.
- shelter: buildings still standing will need to be used for injured, sick, and homeless people
- medical care: any doctors and nurses must be helped by volunteers
- safety: fires need to be put out, and leaking gas pipes or dangerous electricity cables made safe.

Economic Effects

Tsunamis have long-term effects, especially in countries that rely on tourism. In Thailand, the tourist resort Phuket suffered terribly after the 2004 Indian Ocean tsunami. Hotels were only 10 percent full and 80 percent of tourism-related businesses closed, leaving 5,000 people unemployed.

QUIZ: DO YOU KNOW WHAT TO DO?

Now that you have read about tsunamis, do you feel you would have a better chance of survival? Test yourself using this quiz.

1 **What gives you a clue that a tsunami might be going to happen in the next few days?**
   a There is a big storm.
   b There is an increase in minor earthquakes.
   c The weather is suddenly very calm.

2 **You are at the beach and the water suddenly drops to an incredibly low level. What should you do?**
   a Go and investigate: you might never get to see this again without scuba-diving gear.
   b Head for high ground as soon as possible: this is a sign that a tsunami is on its way.
   c Gather your possessions in case you need to run for it later on.

3 **Where is the safest place to shelter from a tsunami?**
   a As far from the shoreline as possible.
   b At the highest, most secure point possible.
   c At the top of the tallest tree you can find.

4 **If your precautions fail and you get caught in the waters of a tsunami, what is your best chance of survival?**
   a Being a really good swimmer.
   b Holding on to something that floats.
   c Clinging to a solid object, such as a lamppost.

5 **What are you most likely to need after a tsunami has struck?**
   a Handheld games console to fill the time until you are rescued.
   b Food, water, and shelter.
   c Your favorite possessions and clothes.

How did you do?

Mostly a or c answers: It would be a good idea to read this book again, and to look at some of the web sites on page 31. At the moment, you'd be lucky to survive a tsunami!

Mostly or all b answers: You would you have a good chance of surviving a tsunami, and might even be able to help other people survive!

DISASTER WATCHING ON THE WEB

Being on disaster watch means being prepared. It also means knowing where to get information ahead of a disaster, knowing how disasters happen, receiving disaster warnings, and getting updates on what is happening after a disaster has struck.

Find out More about Tsunamis

Check out these web sites to find out more about tsunamis.

- **www.howstuffworks.com**

    This site has lots of information about how waves are formed, how tsunamis are formed, and how big waves are tracked and predicted.

- **www.weatherwizkids.com**

    This site has a lot of good information, including a cool animation of how an earthquake causes a tsunami. Key words for searching: earthquake, tsunami, underwater volcano, plate tectonics, seismograph.

- **www.clearlyexplained.com**

    This site has lots of background information about tsunamis, some animated maps, and a great diagram of how a tsunami sensor works.

Tsunamis near you

How would a tsunami affect your local area, and what warning might you get? To find out, contact your local government and see whether:

- they have a tsunami emergency plan, and
- they know of a web site you can look at for tsunami warnings.

Your local library might also be able to help you find this information.

Alternatively, these web sites might be able to steer you toward local information:

- **www.weather.gov/ptwc/** The Pacific Tsunami Warning Center has a live map on its first page, with warnings about events that could cause a tsunami.
- **www.pdc.org** has a live map of current disasters (including earthquakes, volcanoes, floods, and extreme storms), which you can click on to find out more. There is also an excellent resources section, with information about tsunamis and other disasters.

INDEX

A
Africa 6, 8, 13
aftermath 7, 14, 15, 21, 28–29
Alaska 7, 18
animals 15
Atlantic Ocean 6
Australia 16, 19, 21

B
Bangladesh 9

C
Chile 12, 16, 19, 23
coastline shape 6, 7, 13, 15, 19, 21, 23
communications 21

D
damage 5, 6, 7, 9, 14–15, 22, 23, 25
defenses 23
drawback 21, 26, 30
drinking water 14, 29

E
earthquake 4, 5, 6, 7, 8, 9, 12, 16, 17, 18, 19, 22, 30
emergency kit 27
emergency plan 24, 31
environmental impact 14–15
epicenter 9
evacuation 21, 24, 25

F
fault line 9, 12, 17

H
harbor 13, 25
Hawaii 10, 13, 14, 20, 21, 23
high tide 11
human impact 14–15

I
Indian Ocean 6, 7, 18
Indian Ocean tsunami 5, 7, 8, 9, 13, 14, 15, 16, 17, 18, 21, 28, 29
Indonesia 6, 7, 8, 9, 20

J
Japan 5, 7, 16, 17, 18, 23, 27

L
landslides 8

M
Macquarie Island 16
mangrove forests 15
Mediterranean Sea 6
monitoring 17, 19

N
New Zealand 12

P
Pacific islands 7
Pacific Ocean 6, 7, 16, 18, 19, 23
Philippine Sea 6
prediction 16–17
preparation 22

R
reefs 15
relief effort 20
Richter scale 16
run-up 13, 17

S
safety 26, 27, 29
seabed 5, 9, 12, 18
sea level 12, 21, 23
sea walls 23
seismologist 17
seismology 17
Sri Lanka 8, 28
Sumatra 8, 9
Sunda Strait 6
survival 4, 5, 24, 25, 30

T
tectonic plates 8, 12, 17
Thailand 5, 8, 26, 29
trough 12, 13, 21

V
volcano 6, 22, 31

W
warnings 4, 5, 10, 13, 17, 19, 20, 24, 26, 31
water pressure 18, 19